A NOTE FROM THE AUTHOR

Our back garden was the setting for many a great forest adventure. Monsters, wolves and bears were all regular fixtures and if we were lucky enough to make it home alive, my brother, our bestest oldest friends and I would set up camp for the night in the garden. Dad would grapple with our ricketty vintage tent, mum would provide sandwiches and we'd guzzle hot chocolate and chatter excitedly until the sun came up, congratulating ourselves on another most excellent adventure . . .

Florentine and Pig's Spooky Forest Adventure Singalong Song!

Oh how we love to singaling our songalong we do.

We'd love to singaling our Forest Songalong with you.

The sparkling stars are shining and we've got milk malties too!

So bring your friends and join us and let's sing a song or two!

There are twigs and trees and birds and bees and streams and snails to spy.

There are leaves and logs and brooks and bogs and bugs that buzz and fly.

You can see the moon singaling our tune, see the dancing fireflies.

What a whizz bang whizz the forest is, we can't believe our eyes!

You can download the music from our website, so you can toot it on your recorders!

Eva X

Eva Katzler writes the stories

Jess Mikhail draws the pictures

Recipes and crafts by Jess and Laura Tilli

For more recipes, crafts and ideas, please pop over to **www.florentineandpig.com** or become our fan on Facebook — we'd just love to see you there!

Remember, sharp knives and hot things can be dangerous.
Adults should supervise children closely when cooking and crafting.

For my Boshlies. I boshly could not have done it without you – EK

For Sarah Dosanjh – JM

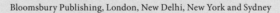

Bloomsbury Publishing, London, New Delhi, New York and Sydney

First published in Great Britain in 2014 by Bloomsbury Publishing Plc
50 Bedford Square, London, WC1B 3DP

Text copyright © Florentine and Pig Ltd 2014
Illustrations copyright © Jess Mikhail 2014
Recipes devised and crafts co-devised by Laura and Jess Tilli
Wallpaper design reproduced by kind permission of Elanbach
The moral rights of the author and illustrator have been asserted

A CIP catalogue record for this book is available from the British Library

ISBN 978 1 4088 2942 4 (HB)
ISBN 978 1 4088 2439 9 (PB)

1 3 5 7 9 10 8 6 4 2

Printed in China by Leo Paper Products, Heshan, Guangdong

www.bloomsbury.com
www.florentineandpig.com
BLOOMSBURY is a registered trademark of Bloomsbury Publishing Plc

Florentine and Pig

and the
Spooky Forest
Adventure

Eva Katzler

Illustrated by Jess Mikhail

Recipes and crafts by Laura and Jess Tilli

BLOOMSBURY

LONDON NEW DELHI NEW YORK SYDNEY

It was a calm, still and quiet night and Florentine and Pig
were tucked up in bed – warm, cosy and sleeping peacefully.

Pig was **snoring** (rather loudly, actually),
and Florentine was **dreaming** something lovely.

socks

pants

There was not a sound in the garden.
Not a sound in the house. Not a pop, not a peep.

When **suddenly** . . .

'Wooooooooooooooooooooooooo!'

Florentine and Pig jumped so high their heads nearly bumped the ceiling!

'Goodness me, Pig!' cried Florentine
'Whatever was **that?**'

Pig peeked out from under the covers,
but before he could blink, there it was again . . .

'WoooooooooooooooooooooooOOOOOOOOO!'

This time was **louder** and **longer** than the time before, and Florentine and Pig leapt into each other's arms!

'Well I never!' Florentine exclaimed.

Florentine and Pig lit a candle, and
held an emergency meeting.

'Now, Pig,' said Florentine, 'We appear to have a
bit of a situation out there.'
Pig nodded, for even though he didn't like to
admit it, Florentine was right.

'Are you thinking what I'm thinking?' she said.
Pig paused. (He found this was always a bit
of a tricky question.)

'That is the sound of . . .

The Growling, prowling BOGMOG!'

Pig gasped.

'The **Growling, Prowling Bog Mog**
lives in the deepest, darkest forest,' whispered
Florentine. 'Have you heard of him, Pig?'

Pig shook his head.
'Well,' said Florentine.
'Listen carefully . . .

He lurks in the bog
In the gloom and fog
The **Growling, Prowling Bog Mog!**

You can hear him wheeze
As he creeps through the trees
The **Growling, Prowling Bog Mog!**

He scowls and he howls
He growls and he prowls
The Growliny, Prowling Bog Mog!

And though he makes a terrible sound
The mysterious monster has never
been found . . .
The Growling, Prowling Bog Mog!

The Growling, Prowling Bog Mog must
never frighten us like that again, Pig,' said
Florentine determinedly.
'We must head into the forest and find him!'

Pig excitedly began loading up his satchel with everything they would need to find the Growling Prowling Bog Mog.

He grabbed their **cosiest** sleeping bags, his **biggest** binoculars, his **brightest** torch, his **warmest** hat, and their camping cooking stove, for they wouldn't want to get hungry, would they?

'Well done, Pig!' said Florentine. 'I've packed us a delicious supper for our adventure—look!'

Pig peeked inside Florentine's knapsack. He could hardly believe his eyes!

♥ Roasty Toasty Campfire Kebobbles

♥ Sunrise Scrambly Eggs
with Tomato Ketchup Soldiers

♥ Sweet Potato Woodland Wedges

♥ Snuggly Buggly Marshmallow Brownies

♥ Star Gazers Stacked Banana Pancakes

♥ Drink-in-Your-Sleeping-Bag
Honey Milk Malties

Pig was feeling hungry already!
Off they marched into the forest.

They **walked** and **talked**, and **trudged** and **tramped**. They **hopped** and **hurdled** through dry and damp.

They **splished** and **splashed** through streams and brooks, They **peeked** through crannies, and **peeped** through nooks.

They searched **down** and **up**, and **in between**. But the Growling, prowling Bog Mog was nowhere to be seen . . .

Suddenly, they heard
a terrible GROAN!
But was it just the wind . . . ?

Then they heard a dreadful
CRACK!
But was it just the
creaky trees . . . ?

And then there was a
WHIIIIIIIISH
and a WHOOOOOOOSH!
But was it just the wild grasses . . . ?

Then, out of nowhere came a loud
GRUMBLE and a RUMBLE . . .

(But that was just the sound of Pig's tummy.)

'I think it's time for supper, Pig,' Florentine giggled.

So they pitched their tent, lit their stove
and ate their **delicious** supper under the stars.

'Oh, Pig, do you think we will ever find the **Growling, prowling Bog Mog?**' said Florentine, glumly.

Pig reached for his guitar and began to play a pretty song. (Pig really does have many hidden talents.)

'What a good idea, Pig,' said Florentine. 'Music always makes me feel so much better.'

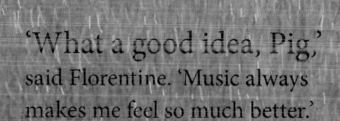

'Oh how we love to singaling our songalong we do . . .'.
We'd love to singaling our Forest Songalong with you . . .'.

Once they had eaten their supper and sung all their songs, Florentine and Pig snuggled down in their sleeping bags and blew out the candle.

They lay there in the dark as quiet as can be with their eyes wide open.
Wondering, waiting, listening.

'Don't worry, Pig,' said Florentine. 'There probably isn't **really** a Growling, Prowling Bog Mog at all. We're just being silly. Now, let's get some sleep.'

Pig closed his eyes, but just as he was drifting off to sleep, there came a very **deep** and **familiar** sound . . .

'Woooooooooooooooooooooooo!'

A dark shadow appeared on their tent . . .
and it was getting bigger,

and bigger,

and bigger!

'Wooooooooooooooooooooo!'

Florentine **quivered** and **quaked**!
Pig bravely stood up.
'What are we going to do, Pig?' she gulped.

His teeth were **clattering** and **chattering**.
His knees were **wibbling** and **wobbling**.

He ever-so-slowly opened the tent
and came face-to-face with . . .

A large . . . feathered . . .
beautiful . . . wide-eyed owl!

'Woooooooooooooooo!'
went the owl, then he flew away
towards the moon.

'Oh, Pig!' Florentine laughed as they tucked themselves back into their sleeping bags.

'Aren't we silly! Of course that wasn't the Growling, prowling Bog Mog. We should have known that it was only a friendly owl!'

Pig nodded off to sleep a happy Pig.
Of **course** it was only the friendly owl . . .

. . . or was it?

The End ...Ta da

Roasty-Toasty Campfire Kebobbles

Makes 4 skewers

You will need

2 courgettes, cut into 2cm chunks
12 cherry tomatoes
12 button mushrooms
Juice of 1 lemon
2 tbsp Olive Oil
1 garlic clove, crushed
Salt and pepper
4 wooden or metal skewers (if wooden
   then soak them in water first)

1 Preheat grill to a medium heat.

2 Pour the oil and lemon juice into your small jug and stir in the garlic, salt and pepper.

3 Gently poke each skewer through alternate vegetables until each one is full up with yummy, colourful veggies.

4 Put the skewers on a plate, pour over the garlicky oil and pop in the fridge overnight, or for at least 25 minutes if you don't have much time.

5 With a grown-up, cook on a hot griddle, a barbeque or under a grill for 10 minutes, turning frequently. Perfect veggie yumminess!

Twinkly Jam Jar Lanterns

You will need
1 jam jar washed and dried
Some coloured or patterned paper
Sticky tape
Scissors
Pipe cleaners
1 tealight candle
Glue and extra sparkles, optional

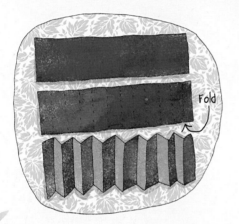

1   Cut your piece of paper into a long strip about the same height as your jam jar, then fold it into a wide concertina fan with each fold about 3cm wide.

2   With your scissors, very carefully cut out some tiny shapes along the folded edges.

3   Unfold your fan and wrap your pretty patterned paper around the jar, securing with sticky tape. You can add extra twinkles and sparkles with glue.

4   Wrap one pipe cleaner around the rim of the jar, and secure by twisting the ends tightly. To make your handle, attach another pipe cleaner to both sides of the jar.

5   Pop your tealight candle inside, get a grown-up to help you light it, and hang your twinkly lantern in your favourite tree! Starry starry night . . .

Magic Shape Shiner

You will need

A small torch
Thin card
Paper
Scissors
Sticky tape
Pencil

Stick with tape

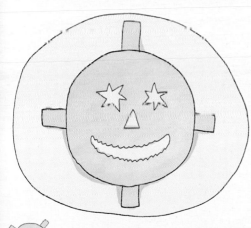

1   Roll your piece of card into a cone, attaching the thin end over your torch light with sticky tape. (You may need an adult pair of hands to help you with this.) Securely fasten the side of your cone with more sticky tape.

2   Draw around the big end of your cone onto a piece of paper. Cut out the circle leaving 1cm around the edge and four tabs to bend and attach the paper to your cone.

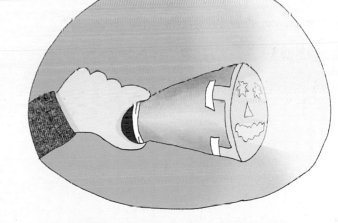

Stick here

Stick here

Stick here

3   Carefully bend your paper circle in half and cut out shapes to make a spooky face.

4   Ask a friend to hold the cone facing upwards so that you can attach the paper circle to the cone, bending over the tabs and securing with sticky tape. The paper circle should completely cover the end of the cone.

5   Turn off the lights and turn on your torch to see your magic shapes shine – they'll look extra magical from the inside of your tent!

Early Sunrise Scrambly Eggs with Tomato Ketchup Soldiers

Makes brekky for two

You will need

4 free range eggs, whisked in a bowl
Handful of grated cheddar
1 spring onion, snipped into small pieces
Salt and pepper
8 cherry tomatoes, halved
Knob of butter
2 slices of wholegrain bread
Tomato ketchup

1 In a frying pan melt the butter on a gentle heat.

2 Add the eggs, spring onions, cheese and tomatoes, and mix gently with a wooden spoon for about two minutes until firm. Add a pinch of salt and pepper.

3 Toast the bread and squirt with ketchup in a squiggly pattern. Cut each piece of toast into five ketchupy soldiers.

4 Spoon a big pile of the eggy mixture onto each plate and arrange the soldiers around the edge. Scrambly scrumminess!

Sweet Potato Woodland Wedges with Rosemary and Garlic Mayo

Wedges for 6 campers

You will need

4 medium sweet potatoes, scrubbed
Olive Oil
Salt and pepper
4 tbsp mayonnaise
1 clove garlic, crushed
2 tsp chopped fresh rosemary leaves

1 Preheat your oven to 180°C/350°F/ Gas mark 4.

2 Carefully chop your potatoes in half then slice each half into four.

3 Put them onto a baking tray, drizzle with olive oil and sprinkle with a little salt and pepper. Pop into the oven for 45 minutes until golden.

4 Mix the garlic and rosemary into the mayonnaise, and tip into a little bowl. Decorate with a sprig of rosemary. Dip the hot wedges into the yummy mixture . . . happy tummies all round!

Snuggly Buggly Marshmallow Brownies

Makes 12 brownies

You will need

150g butter
150g plain flour
300g soft brown sugar
100g milk chocolate
100g plain chocolate
2 tbsp cocoa
4 eggs, beaten
200g marshmallows, chopped in half

1. Preheat your oven to 180ºC/350ºF/ Gas mark 4.

2. Carefully melt the chocolate and butter together in a bowl over a pan of simmering water.

3. In a big bowl, mix together all of the other ingredients apart from the marshmallows and stir in your melted chocolate mixture.

4. Carefully stir in most of the marshmallows, then tip the mixture into a lined baking tray. Scatter the rest of the marshmallows on top. Pop into your hot oven for 20 minutes.

5. When ready, the mixture should be set on top but wobbly underneath. Leave to cool then chop up and share with your bestest campfire friends.

Star Gazers' Stacked Banana Pancakes with Oozy Golden Syrup

For two friends

You will need

100g self raising flour
1 tbs soft brown sugar
1 egg, beaten
100ml milk
2 ripe bananas, mashed
1 banana, sliced
Oil for frying
Golden syrup

1. In a big bowl, mix together the flour, sugar, egg, milk and mashed banana until you have a lumpy bumpy batter.

2. Heat a tablespoon of oil in a pan and pour in the batter to make small pancake shapes (about the size of a large biscuit).

3. Cook the pancakes for about two minutes on each side until they are golden brown and starting to go crispy.

4. Layer the little pancakes up on a plate with the sliced banana between each one and drizzle with the golden syrup while the pancakes are still warm. Oozy deliciousness!

Drink-in-your-Sleeping-Bag Honey Milk Malties

You will need
4 mugfuls of milk
2 tbsp honey
A pinch of cinnamon
Squirty cream
2 small bags of Maltesers

1. Warm the milk in a saucepan over a gentle heat, stirring constantly. Stir in the honey and cinnamon.

2. Carefully crush one packet of Maltesers with a rolling pin or baked bean tin, and add to your milk mixture.

3. Divide between four mugs, add some squirty cream in a spiral shape and scatter the rest of the Maltesers on top. Best Midnight Feast EVER!